SYDNEY CARLSON

Racism STOPS with Me

A Pledge of Intention for Elementary School Children and their Adult Leaders

Copyright © 2022 Sydney Carlson.
Cover illustration by Saidi Alifa.
All Rights Reserved.

ISBN: 978-1-326-25044-7

Names, characters, places, and incidents are either products of the author/'s imagination or, if real, are used fictitiously. No part of this publication may be reproduced, distributed, or transmitted in any form or by any means, including photocopying, recording, or other electronic or mechanical methods, without the prior written permission of the author.

Limelight Publishing
Po Box 45, Kallangur
Queensland, Australia, 4503
www.limelightpublishing.com

Lulu Press
PO Box 12018
Durham, NC 27709
United States
www.lulu.com

www.lulu.com
www.limelightpublishing.com

Quantity sales. Special discounts are available on quantity purchases by corporations, associations, and others. For details, contact the publisher at the address above.

This pledge is dedicated to my mother Diedra Carlson
who has fought tirelessly for the rights of all students in her care,
even when the system of racial hierarchy has attempted to silence her.
Thank you for showing me how to make "good trouble".
Excelsior!

About the Illustrator

Saidi Alifa is a freelance digital illustrator based in Blantyre, Malawi. Having always had a knack for drawing, Saidi spent a better part of his childhood doodling on anything he could get his hands on. It was in 2019 that he decided to turn professional and take his craft to the next level. His illustrations are semi realistic, and include the use of bold lines and harmonious colors, that mesh together to capture moments that tell stories.

Introduction to the Pledge

For Adult Leaders:

Hello, and welcome! I assume you picked this book because you would like to raise antiracist students/children. I hope so because we need all the help we can get. If you feel prepared to take on this task, I need you to do a couple of things before or alongside reading this pledge to wee babes.

Number One: Ask yourself how far you are in your personal antiracist journey. Have you started to read books by non-white authors (not my book, but like grown-up adult books with big words, ya know)? Have you spoken to your family/ friends/ colleagues about race? Have you "called in" anyone when they have intentionally or unintentionally used racist language or tropes? It's alright if you said no to some or all of these things (it is not an exhaustive list), but if antiracism is important to you- you picked this book, so I believe it is- reflect on what you have done to SHOW your commitment. Children can smell frauds from a mile away, and the authenticity you have with your practice will show them that antiracism and allyship is a journey, not a destination. Children will appreciate your perspective if they know it is honest.

Number Two: This practice requires work. As you guide children through this process, remember that your journey does not end. If you have been waiting to have a conversation about race, have it. If you keep hearing and seeing racial injustice, call it out. If I am the first author of color you have listened to, go and seek more. Race intersects with so many other complex identities and experiences, and while this pledge focuses on antiracist work, the primary intent is to celebrate our bold, beautiful, unique, complete selves. Take time to hear the FULL dynamic stories from those willing to share about their intersectional identities and thank them, vocally and monetarily, for their contributions to your learning. Make mistakes (I make mine hourly) and own up to the hurt you've caused.

This takes patience and perseverance, but I promise I am rooting for you.

For the Youth:

Hello Learners and Leaders,

You are about to hear and learn a pledge. How many of you know what a pledge is? It is okay if you don't. There are many ways to describe a pledge, but I like to think of it as a way to be mindful. Being mindful is like being aware. Some of you may be aware of racism. Some of you may have heard the word racism but may not know what it means. Some of you may not know what I am talking about at all. Wherever you are at right now is okay, but before we get started, I want you all to understand some important words in, or about, our pledge.

Racism - Racism is when one person (or a group) who has power treats people unfairly for the color of their skin or their cultural background. Being a White person in many parts of the world can hold a lot of power. Who has power in your space right now? Do you have the same power as people in your space? How is it the same? How is it different?

Antiracism - Antiracism is understanding and working to end racism. Who do you know that is trying to end racism? How do they do it? What can you do to help end racism?

Ally - An ally is someone who works with you to solve a problem. This person uses words and actions to make the world a better, safer place. Allies come in all shapes and sizes, but the one thing they have in common is taking action against something wrong. In your life, who is an ally? What actions do they take to help make the world better?

Vow - A vow is a very strong promise. If someone vows to do something, they are promising to do it.

Race - Race is a way to separate people by how they look, where they come from and how they act. If someone were to ask you "what race are you?", how would you respond?

Every day when I awake
I make a pledge I vow to take

That everyone all day I see
Is no better or worse than me

I vow to see your color
I vow to understand your race

I vow to honor your differences
I vow to respect your space

SCIENCE
WORLD MAP
CONTINENTS
Daily 5
WORKING HARD
BLACK HISTORY
MALCOM X
Be Kind

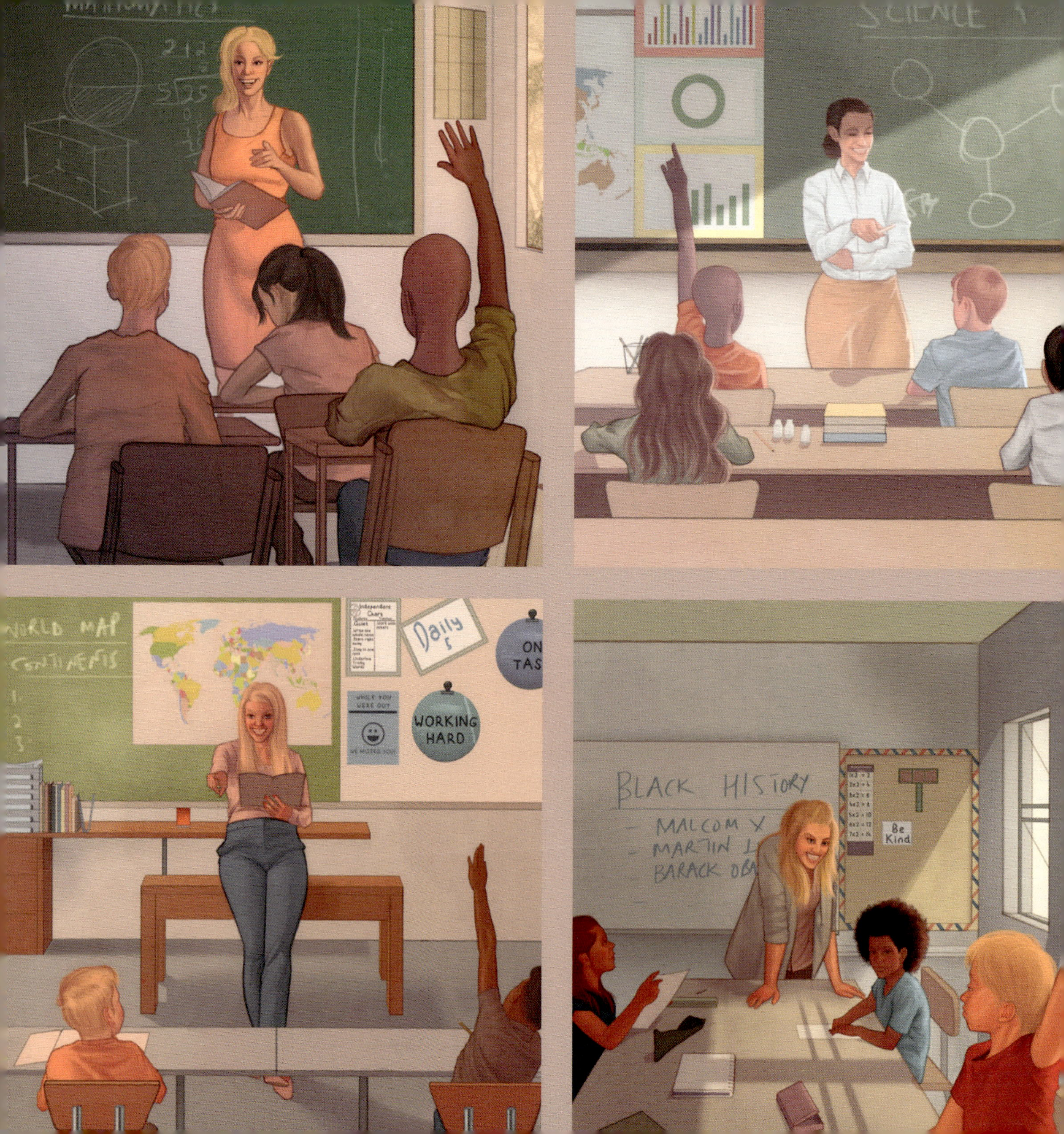

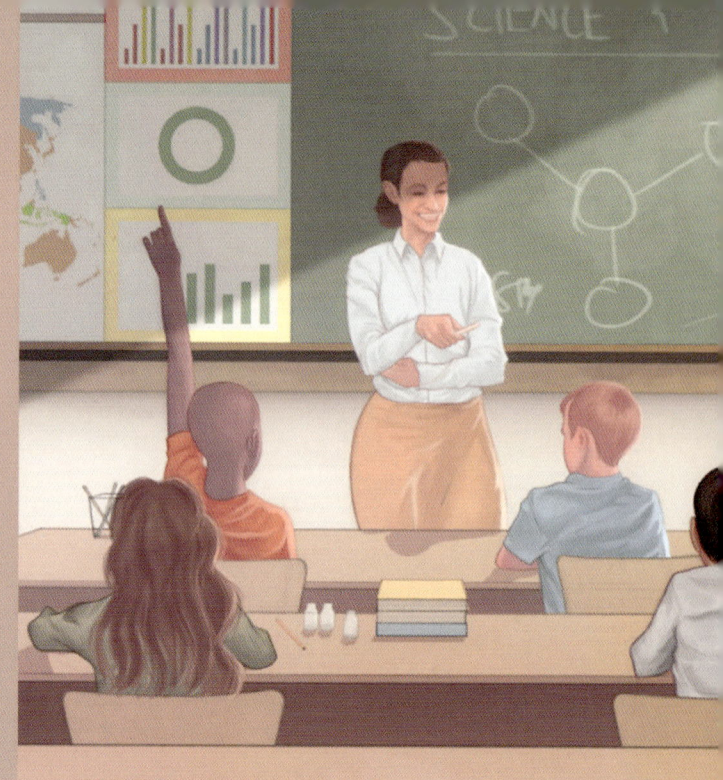

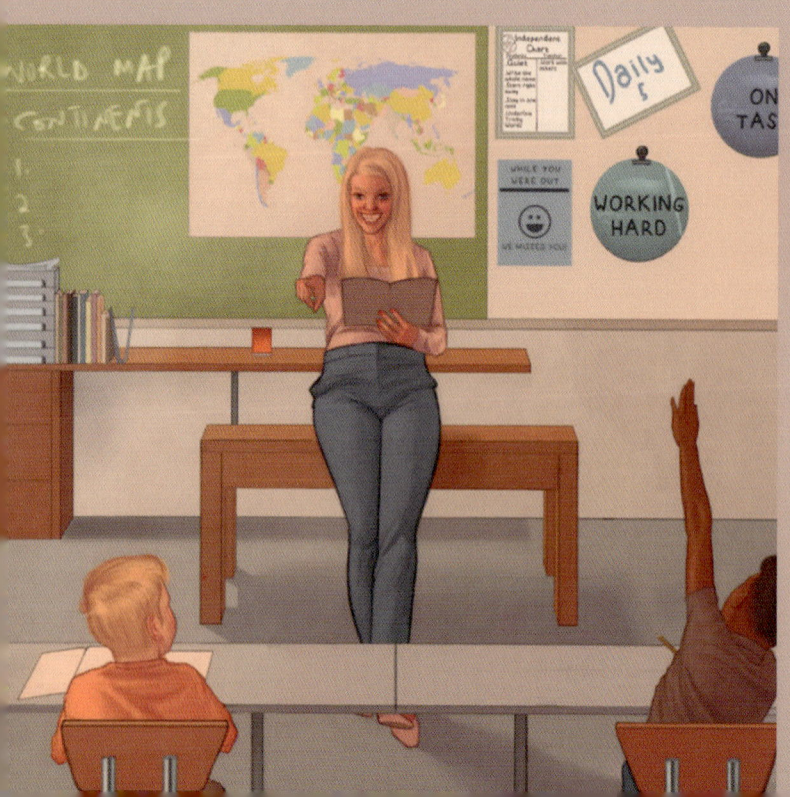

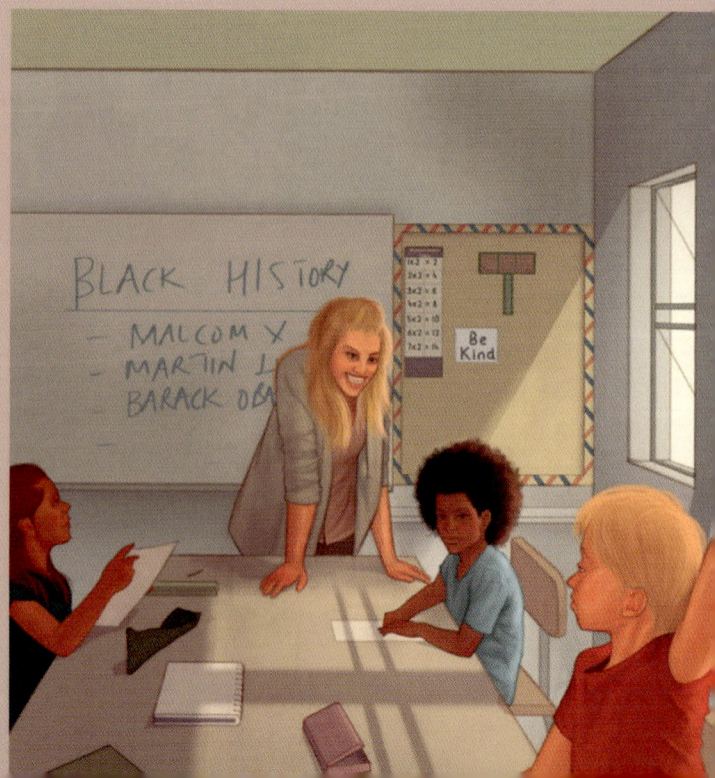

When I see racism
Or act in a racist way

I promise to apologize
And learn from you everyday

I understand that what I know
could be challenged
and hurt I might be

But I vow to stay educated and aware

Because racism STOPS with me

Reflection Questions

1. What do you wonder after hearing this pledge?

2. What stood out to you in the words of the pledge? What stood out to you from the pictures?

3. Pick a picture in the book. What do you notice? What do you wonder?

4. There are many different skin colors in this book. Are any of the skin colors like yours? How would you describe your skin color?

5. Do you have friends that look different from you? How do you talk about the differences between you and your friends?

6. Has anyone treated you or someone you know differently because of how they look? How did that make you feel? Why did you feel that way?

7. Have you ever treated someone differently because of how they look? How do you think it made them feel? Why do you think it made them feel that way?

8. What is racism? How would you explain racism to your family and friends?

9. We're not always right. When you've caused harm, what do you do to repair?

10. How do you make a vow to end racism today?